For Emily & Max

Copyright © 2020 by Jashar Awan

Printed in China
First Edition

For information about permission to reproduce selections from this book, write to
Permissions, W. W. Norton & Company, Inc., 500 Fifth Avenue, New York, NY 10110

For information about special discounts for bulk purchases, please contact
W. W. Norton Special Sales at specialsales@wwnorton.com or 800-233-4830

Library of Congress Cataloging-in-Publication Data

Names: Awan, Jashar, author, illustrator.
Title: What a lucky day! / by Jashar Awan.
Description: First edition. | New York, NY : W. W. Norton & Company, [2020]
| Audience: Ages 4–8. | Summary: Four animals make their way to a pier, hoping to catch some fish for dinner,
but as they spy one another each fears another will ruin his or her luck.
Identifiers: LCCN 2020004083 | ISBN 9781324015529 (hardcover) | ISBN 9781324015536 (epub)
Subjects: CYAC: Luck—Fiction. | Fishing—Fiction. | Animals—Fiction.
Classification: LCC PZ7.1.A976 Wh 2020 | DDC [E]—dc23
LC record available at https://lccn.loc.gov/2020004083

W. W. Norton & Company, Inc., 500 Fifth Avenue, New York, N.Y. 10110
www.wwnorton.com

W. W. Norton & Company Ltd., 15 Carlisle Street, London W1D 3BS

1 2 3 4 5 6 7 8 9 0

WHAT A LUCKY DAY!

Jashar Awan

NORTON YOUNG READERS

An Imprint of W. W. Norton & Company • Independent Publishers Since 1923

I'm going fishing today.
If I'm lucky, I'll have
fish for dinner.

I won't catch
anything today!

I'm going
fishing today.
If I'm lucky, I'll have
fish for dinner.

OH NO! A RACCOON!
That masked bandit
will steal my fish!

I'm going fishing today.
If I'm lucky, I'll have
fish for dinner.

OH NO! A FROG!
I hope I don't get warts!

**I'm fishing today.
If I'm lucky, I'll have
fish for dinner.**

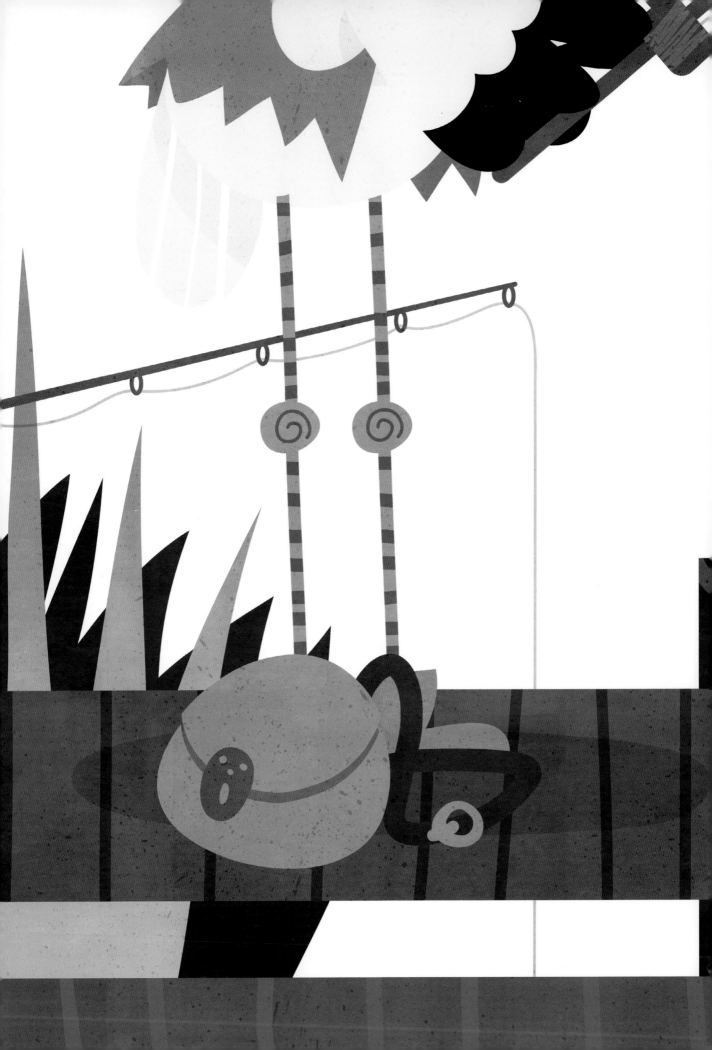

OH NO! A STORK!
I hope he doesn't
deliver any babies!
This pier is crowded
enough already.

WHAT A LUCKY DAY!

WHAT A LUCKY DAY!

You were not bad luck after all, Black Cat!

Bad luck?
Why would I be bad luck?

Oh! I'd always heard black cats brought bad luck.

Excuse me.

**Warts are caused
by a virus.
Not by me.**

FISH DINNER!

Hooray!

**Eat up!
There's enough
for everyone!**

**Yeah! We're
lucky Stork
didn't deliver
any babies!**

Wait. What?

Why would I deliver babies?

WAIT.
WHAT?

Thieves wear masks so no one will know who they are, but a **raccoon**'s mask-like fur has a very different purpose. The dark markings around their eyes help raccoons see at night by absorbing light. Raccoons are nocturnal—they sleep all day and stay up all night! The raccoon's mask and its nocturnal habits have contributed to its reputation as a bandit.

Warts are small growths on the skin caused by the human papillomavirus (HPV). While some **frogs** and toads have bumps that look like warts, they don't carry this particular virus. Make sure to wash your hands with soap after touching a frog, though—frogs won't give you warts but they can carry bacteria or toxins!